D0460631

Under the Lilacs

E. B. GOODALE

Houghton Mifflin Harcourt | Boston | New York

Sometimes I want to run away.

When Mom teaches flute
lessons once a week, she shuts the
door and says, "Play nice with your sister."

Hannah shuts the door
to our room and says, “I’m busy”
and “find somewhere else to play.”

I write a note to let Mom know that I'm leaving and she will never see me again.

I wait for her to come running.

I wait and wait and wait.

Will anyone notice that I'm gone?

Maybe I could live here, under the lilacs.

All I need are some sticks and cardboard to build a roof. These rocks will work as a porch.

My pen pal could still write me letters as long as I let him know my new address.

These strawberries should last me through
the winter if I save them.

I just have to train Mango to come in the back way so that our neighbor doesn't bark at her . . .

. . . and she can sleep on my pillow like always.

I think Mango might miss Hannah,
so I should probably make a room for her.

But there is not much space, so we could share my room.

I think Mango might also miss Mom,
so I should probably make a room for her too.

She could even teach her flute lessons in here.

SOLOS
FOR
FLUTE

Yes, I think I could stay here, under the lilacs.

At least for a little while.

For Mom . . . and Mango.

hmhbooks.com

The illustrations for this book were made using monoprinting, ink, and digital collage.
The text type was set in Bembo Book MT Std.
The display type was set in Garden Pro.

Designed by Whitney Leader-Picone

Library of Congress Control Number: 2019007479

ISBN: 978-0-358-15393-1

Manufactured in China
SCP 10 9 8 7 6 5 4 3 2 1
4500785153